Dark Sparkle Tea

and Other Bedtime Poems

Sagittarius

Tonight when I gazed across the sky,
I saw a teapot made of stars
a-pouring tea from its starry spout
into the upturned crescent moon

as if it weren't the moon at all
but a china cup of pale gold:
and oh for a starry drink of that,
for a sip of that dark-sparkle tea!

Tim Myers

Illustrated by
Kelley Cunningham

WORDSONG • Boyds Mills Press

To Molly, Emma, Ben, Luke, Matt, Claire, Daniel, Joe, Jack, Josh, Jake, Sam, Jacob, Cody, Alex, Hayden, Mitch, Tess, Hank, Clayton, Melissa, Matt (a different one), Shannon, Mike, Mark, Joe (a different one), Maggie, and Jonathan—believe it or not, my nieces and nephews!

—T. M.

To Sam, Noah, and Nathaniel, the joys of my life

— K. C.

Text copyright © 2006 by Tim Myers
Illustrations copyright © 2006 by Kelley Cunningham
All rights reserved

Published by Boyds Mills Press, Inc.
A Highlights Company
815 Church Street
Honesdale, Pennsylvania 18431
Printed in China

CIP data is available

First edition, 2006
The text is set in 12-point Caxton Light.
The illustrations are done in pastel.

Visit our Web site at www.boydsmillspress.com

10 9 8 7 6 5 4 3 2 1

Table of Contents

Silly Night Song

Oh, with a *dong* and a *ding*
as the big clock sings,
we're dripping and done,
tubbed and towel-rubbed,
now jumping in jammers,
like bed-bound jackhammers,

then once we've had snack and go back
wanting more, and a long drippy drink
and have gone to the bathroom
(whether we had to or not, to be sure!)
and the story's all through, *boo-hoo*,

then each little slug-a-bed lying so snug abed
getting our last little kiss and sweet hug abed,
each of us now a snooze-worthy dervish,
sleepy-eyed, floppy-down, Do-Not-Disturb-ish,
clutching as much of stuffed critters as can,

each weary llama cuddled by Mama,
popped under covers by Papa,
toasty and tired, tucked ever so tightly—

just then, every nightly,
is when it begins—
that music from chins,
that slumber-deep ease:

those whole
symphonies
of

z's

Just Five Minutes More

"It's time for bed! It's time for bed!"
My mom and dad go out of their heads
when the clock on the wall has quietly said,
It's eight o'clock and time for bed.

They say I'll be grumpy tomorrow
if I don't sleep deep tonight.
And I suppose . . . I am kind of tired. . . .
Maybe—just maybe—they're right. . . .

So I think I'll invent an invention:
a living-room rocket-sled
that will streak down tracks in the hallway
and fling me into my bed—

I'd be there in less than a second,
tucked in and ready to snore.
So when bedtime came I'd have time to play
for JUST FIVE MINUTES MORE!

Sleepwalker

Neddie DeRev
got up from his bed,
walked out of the house
with dreams in his head,

for hours and hours
tramped through the town,
short streets and long streets,
up hill and down.

At last growing tired
of wandering and seeking,
he came to his school just as
daylight was peeking,

walked into his classroom,
sat down at his desk.
The teacher came in,
gave a cry of distress,

said, "Neddie, my word,
you've come early this morning!"
Ned said, "Time for bed,"
dropped his head, started snoring.

Bedtime Song

Cattle mooing low, say
low now, slow now,
cattle mooing low,
I say.

Rain on the roof, say
tap now, drum now,
rain on the roof,
I say.

Blue in the candle flame,
quiver now, shiver now,
blue in the flame,
I say.

Bells in the town, say
bong now, clong now,
bells in the town,
I say.

Couple hundred countries, say
big world, wide world,
couple hundred countries,
I say.

Slow-going traveler, say
left foot, right foot,
slow-going traveler,
I say.

End of the journey, say
warm bed, soft bed,
end of the journey,
I say.

9

Bees at Night

When the dizzy busy buzzy bees
come home to their hive at night,
bee-yawning beyond the fields
where they waggle-worked all day,

they climb through the winding hidden hive
to their cozy, dozy beds, and then—
oh not a bizz of a buzz there is,
not a wheeze or a sneeze

as bee dreams come
of work to be done, of honey and sun.
And the queen at the heart of the hive? She dreams
of her thousands of daughters and sons.

The June moon shines, the world is still,
hollyhocks closed in their rows on the hill,
and the dreaming bees are at ease
as cool night breezes breeze—

and oh, this pleases the bees,
all blissful and buzzless in bed,
as they lie with shut eyes, like stars in the skies,
bee dreams abuzz in their heads.

HONEY
SAFE

Listening to Cricket Nick

At night,
listen close—
it's there
on the air,
loud enough
if you're quiet:
that's Cricket Nick singing.

In bed,
listen hard—
for down
in the yard,
all night long
the song
that Cricket Nick's bringing.

In the dark,
listen now—
he's played
half the day,
takes a bow,
then goes on
to the deep night's middle:

Lively hands
on the frets,
hear it go,
little tune
white as moon:
Cricket Nick
as he sings to his fiddle.

At the Skunks' House

What does the skunk mother say
at the close of day,
when her little ones' black-and-white heads
are all nodding?

"Come, little stinkhearts
so darling and foul,
it's off to your bushy-tail beds
and no dawdling.

"Come, my dear stenchlings,
so cute and sharp-scented,
my precious wee Limburgers
rank and well-vented—

"Come and wash faces, both black fur and white.
Come kiss your papa and mama good-night.
Come, you fine stinkbugs, all cuddly and smelly,
and I'll ruffle your heads and scratch your dear bellies,

"Then into pajamas and off to your rooms,
little heads to your beds and the air full of fumes.
Pew, sour-bottoms! And now not a wink.
And remember we're proud of how badly you stink!"

13

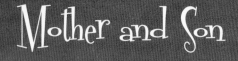

Mother and Son

The mother has seen the world.
Her young son studies the globe.
She's happy to live at home again;
he thinks of the tales she's told.

"Did you really go to Paris?"
"What was it like in Japan?"
"Tell me that story about Peru!"
She smiles and tells it again.

That night, when both are sleeping,
she dreams of a garden, a lawn,
of flowers beside a house; he dreams
of maps and a ship at dawn.

Father to Child

Did I ever tell you the starry story
of how you first came into our lives?
That night I was out in the yard, looked up
just as a star came blurring down,

and I could see where it was headed,
the bright arc of that shooting star,
so I ran for my first-baseman's mitt,
went charging down the street.

I sprinted, legs churning, heart racing,
like a big-leaguer breaking for the outfield fence,
and closer, closer, the star streaking down,
so close now, so wild-shining, I could feel

its heat on my face. At the last second
I jumped, straining, my arm stretched out—
and I heard that star go *plop*! right in the pocket
as I landed flat on the neighbor's lawn.

And then I sat up, my heart still pounding,
slowly opened the mitt, and there
was the tiniest, most precious, sky-fallen baby,
still half-covered with stardust . . .

It was you.

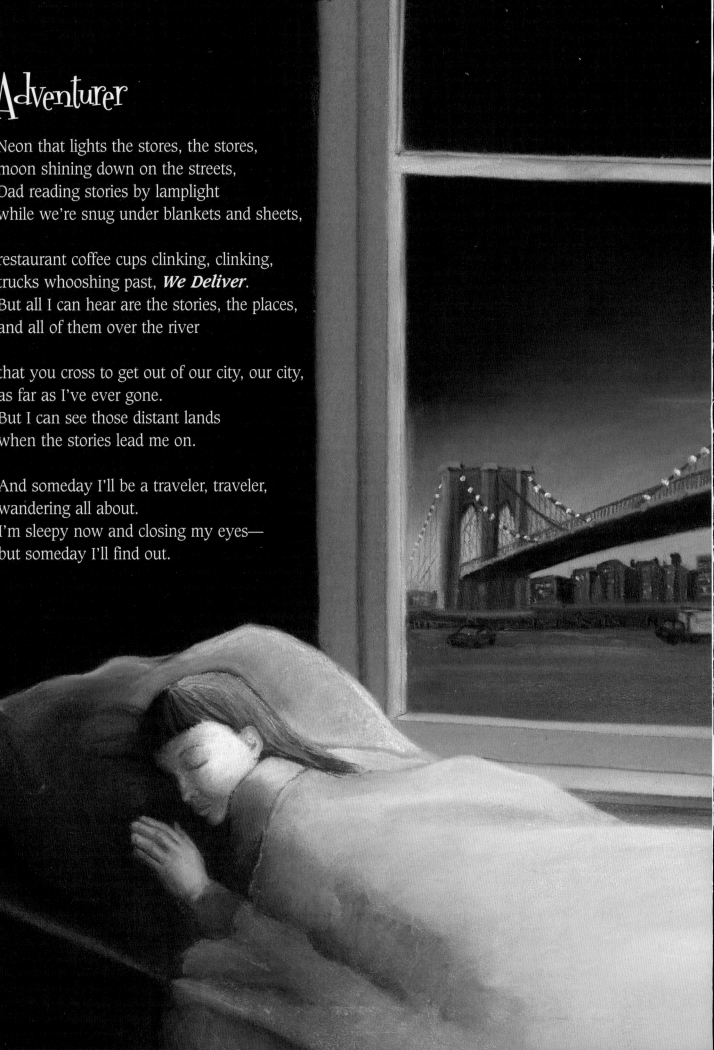

Adventurer

Neon that lights the stores, the stores,
moon shining down on the streets,
Dad reading stories by lamplight
while we're snug under blankets and sheets,

restaurant coffee cups clinking, clinking,
trucks whooshing past, **We Deliver**.
But all I can hear are the stories, the places,
and all of them over the river

that you cross to get out of our city, our city,
as far as I've ever gone.
But I can see those distant lands
when the stories lead me on.

And someday I'll be a traveler, traveler,
wandering all about.
I'm sleepy now and closing my eyes—
but someday I'll find out.

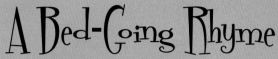

A Bed-Going Rhyme

Nonny nonny nussknocker
Nonny nonny noo
In came their mother saying
I love you

Nonny nonny nussknocker
Nonny nonny ned
Popped them in their jamas and it's
off to bed

Nonny nonny nussknocker
Nonny nonny nore
Read them a story but
they want one more

Nonny nonny nussknocker
Nonny nonny nink
Can't fall asleep till
they've had a drink

Nonny nonny nussknocker
Nonny nonny nile
Mom, will you sit in the chair
for a while?

Nonny nonny nussknocker
Nonny nonny neep
Bouncing on their beds 'cause
Mom fell asleep!

18

Putting the Baby to Sleep

Yap, baby, yap—
you'll never take your nap.
You'd rather yelp and drool instead,
bounce your crib toys off my head—
So yap, baby, yap.

Shout, baby, shout—
the dog is running out.
The cat is running close behind.
They seem to think you're Frankenstein—
so shout, baby, shout.

Howl, baby, howl—
you screech worse than an owl.
You're fed and changed; it's all been done—
I think you're screaming just for fun!
So howl, baby, howl.

Cry, baby, cry—
you'll never close your eyes.
I'll be here for a hundred years
with you still shrieking in my ears—

Hey!

She's asleep!

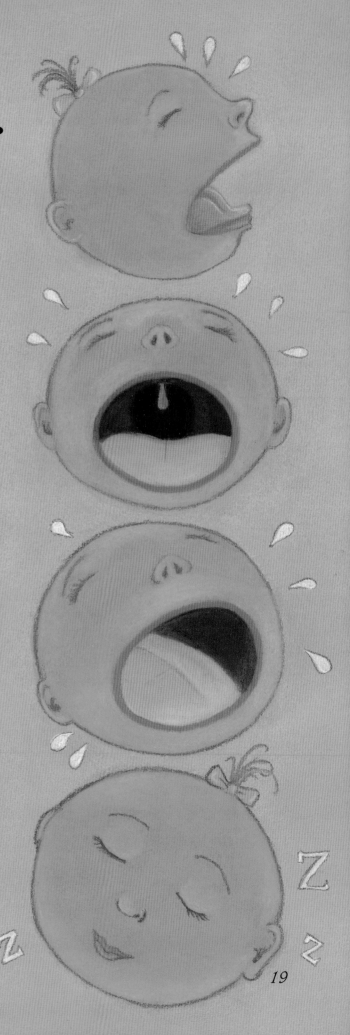

19

Frisky Freaks Out

Once I woke at three a.m.
to a wild, high-pitched noise
that seemed to come from my hamster's cage
in the corner by my toys.

So I trained my camping flashlight
on his wheel and cedar shavings—
and I couldn't believe my eyes
when I saw how he was behaving.

My hamster was a rock star!
He was wearing spangled tights!
He was crashing his paw on a tiny guitar
surrounded by flashing lights!

His fur was yellow and green and red
and spiked around his ears!
He danced around in little boots
and wiggled his furry rear!

He was singing "Baby, baby!
You the one I need!"
He was screaming "Oooh, you drive me crazy,
sweet little sunflower seed!"

But things are different now. Imagine—
a hamster rocking till dawn!
I had to get tough. Now I make him
play with his headphones on.

Night Visitor

One night a lion came out
of the picture on my shelf.
I woke up when he growled a bit
and had to pinch myself.

He lifted one enormous paw
and set it on my shoulder.
I felt his claws, as long as nails—
and I scooted over.

But then he lay down next to me
and started snuggling up.
I held my breath—but he was warm
and harmless as a pup.

Soon he fell asleep, his big chest
lifting up and down,
and so I slowly drifted off
to his breathing sounds.

When I woke up that morning,
I was all alone in bed.
But I could see the lion
when I sat and turned my head:

a picture once again, who'd slept
beside me like a brother—
gentle as a lamb, and didn't even
steal the covers.

If You Feel Lonely

If you feel lonely in your bed,
then don't forget, dear sleepyhead,
that while you lie there, all around
the Others too are lying down:

wolves with tails across their noses;
bees who dream of morning roses;
squirrels rocking high in trees;
camels settling to their knees;

whale calves beside their mothers
with the ocean waves for covers;
wombats, pandas, kinkajous,
each deliciously a-snooze;

birds with heads beneath their wings;
mother bat as baby clings;
rabbits in their winter burrows
dreaming there beneath the furrows . . .

If you feel lonely in your bed,
then don't forget, my sleepyhead:
all night long, as darkness lulls,
you're sleeping with the Animals.

23

What the Dad Said to His Kids at 8:23 on a School Night

All right, you rambling roustabouts,
you leaping, quirking, twitching, ever-itching little rebel rodents—
get your waggly buns to bed!
It's getting late! Don't make me wait!
Every bleary little dear of you has a date
with the Sandman—no handstands, headstands, cartwheels—
don't streel about, you sluggy bugs!
Don't reel and shout! Don't quake and beg!
Just shake those lazy legs down the hall, one and all,
even if you have to crawl
or clamber or trudge or roll or hop or sprint or lope
or slither on your bellies like reptiles!
Better motor-vate your tiny hinder acres.
That's right—move those little gonder-shakers!
No, my flitting flying folk, no more playing, daying, staying up!
Into the sack, every last pup!

Just get quickly, slickly, untrickily under covers, lovers,
no buts about it—knocked out, in deep,
crashed and stashed, conked and zonked,
beautifully, blamelessly blacked out and blissfully dream-chasing!
Lids down and sleepy town, you pillow pirates!
I want it as quiet in here as
bats in their daytime swaytime all hung snug.
I want you all sawing logs, making z's,
punching in for your shift at the snooze factories,
eyes shut tight to your little nightlight, dreams in sight.

Now, is everyone tucked in—covers to chin—
pillows fluffed—had enough?

What?—What's that?

Oh, all right. I'll tell you a story.

My Brother and Me

We climb the stairs, my brother and me,
and settle into our beds.
But I can't stop the thinking and wondering
whirling through my head.

My mom says, "close your eyes," but colors
and funny shapes appear,
and they rush around and glow and fade . . .
But slowly my mind comes clear,

and then, when I'm quiet and falling asleep,
I suddenly, dreamingly, see
otters asleep on the ocean,
bears in a fallen tree.

The otters have wrapped themselves in kelp
to keep from drifting far;
the bears have curled up close beneath
those frosty winter stars.

Like otters on waters, my brother and me,
like bears in their lairs asleep,
quiet and safe and dreaming
like otters a-snooze on the deep.

A Burglar Came on Saturday Night

A burglar came on Saturday night,
creeping when the moon was bright,
with all of the family sleeping like logs—
and we'd forgotten to feed our dog.

I mention this error simply because
a hungry dog gets itchy jaws,
and dogs of course are not that keen
on missing meals that should have been.

The dog was sleeping by the door.
The burglar tiptoed over the floor.
The dog was dreaming of T-bone steak
and suddenly found himself awake . . .

That burglar learned his lesson well,
for there, without a tune,
he danced a dance by the seat of his pants,
he danced by the light of the moon.

And then he ran away, and I don't
think he's coming back—
not after Fido chose his rumpus
for a midnight snack!

Invitation to Dream

When I was the only one in that magic palace,
I sang to my echoes along the halls of marble,
slept at night in the down of the royal featherbed,
my blanket the King's red silken banner.

I bathed in a blue-green, bright-tiled tub so big
my frogs couldn't hop from one end to the other,
then feasted on chocolate and strawberries down in the pantry,
drank the sweetest wine from the deepest cellars.

When sun came in like fire on the polished floors,
I dipped a crown in soap-water to make bubbles.
I rode every horse in the stables, gave them oats,
fed the deer with almonds and primrose petals.

Sometimes at night in the dark of the moon I'd climb
with the King's best fireworks up to his highest tower,
shoot them off till all the sky was dazzling
and sparks of every color fell in showers.

No one ever said no to me, not once.
I played the hundred music boxes whenever
I wanted. Tonight I'm going back—I'll dream again.
You dream it too, so we can go together.

A Wish

I wish I could see,
as night comes on,
how the deer who hide
all day long

are not so shy
when shadows come,
hungry enough
not to turn and run,

but step from the trees,
nervous and peering—
then lower their heads
and feed in the clearing.

For Star-Watchers

If ever you're up on a winter night
and under the open sky,
I promise you a stirring sight
as darkness wheels by:

For there in the south in winter,
as constellations arc,
the Hunting Dog and the Hunter
are tracking through the dark.

Canis is the dog's name;
the hunter is Orion.
They go together, always moving
toward the far horizon.

Canis runs through frosty air,
leaps and barks and plays.
He pants in puffs of icy white
that make the Milky Way.

Orion strides before him
through star-grass fields above,
hopes to fill the cooking pot
to feed the ones he loves.

Across the star-bespangled length
of darkness you will find them:
the hunter joyous in his strength,
his bounding dog behind him.

Halcyon
(Another Name for the Kingfisher Bird)

Long ago, the old folks say,
kingfishers would build
their nests upon the winter sea—
and then the sea was stilled.

Tonight, dear one, I tuck you in,
and I'll be sure to see
that you stay safe and cozy here,
sleeping peacefully.

I'll be like the bird, you be
the birdling in its nest;
we'll drift all night upon the swells
and bring the ocean rest.